I BECAME
KAREN
OVERNIGHT!

(1st of a set of 7 books)

KAREN SMITH

Published in the United States of America

Brilliant Books Literary
137 Forest Park Lane Thomasville
North Carolina 27360 USA

ISBN:
Paperback: 979-8-88945-376-5
Ebook: 979-8-88945-377-2

ACKNOWLEDGEMENTS

A huge thank you to my children for putting up with and supporting my unique ideas based on my extraordinary experiences. Sometimes it has been hard I know to understand my vision. But you always continued to trust in the process. Thank you to Mr Henderson who has always believed in me and who has constantly supported me being a writer knowing that I would be able to share my gifts to the world one day.

CHAPTER 1

It was early in the morning and Karen could feel the chills of the open window on her naked skin. The water running down her back and the hairs standing up on her neck. It was happening again, the thing, was here. Not only was he here but he came to collect his debt and she knew she had to bleed this time to satisfy the demon. For only blood would have him crawling back to the pit of hell. Karen walked to the window and tapped on the glass 3 times 1......2......3. He answered, "you know I am here Karen, interesting!" He was in a good mood today. *Can demons really be in a good mood,*" she thought. The image of him, is he a him or a thing? It was difficult to tell sometimes for he came to her in many forms. Sometimes as a thing, an animal. Sometimes he came as a human, and sometimes he just came as nothing. The nothingness, she felt at those times, makes it hard to look at herself most days.

"Karen!" the thing called. "I have been waiting for you to tell me why I am here!" he snarls.

Karen sat down before she answered getting ready for what is to come. "To collect my blood. I must bleed this time right," Karen said, trembling from the cold water dripping from her skin.

"This time and every time or you know what will happen. Just a little blood it will not hurt you, your father gave you plenty right." The demon was taunting her now.

"I already told you there is no God! No God exist here!" Karen was angry. "No God exists!"

"Whatever you say Karen. No God exists!" The demon mocked her.

"Anyway take it and leave, now! You are making me angry!" Karen was bored of the ritual, she wanted it over and done with, she had seen enough of him or it.

"I think it is a little late for that don't you think, Karen. You already sound angry." He cut her at the neck before she could answer back. As the blood dripped from her he sucked each drop wishing he could rip the skin from her body. Get to what he truly wanted to consume which was her soul, but that would have to wait for another day. The devil was waiting for an answer to the question. Is she going to give up her soul anytime soon? Has she had enough of the cruel reality that she stood in. The World that she lived in filled with the monsters people could only not hope to imagine was real. But here she stood living in it, fighting for it. Not knowing what day was going to be her last. For how long was the devil going to wait at bay accepting the deal, the deal he had tried to break many times. No one can truly trust the devil can they. Who ever heard of a trustworthy devil after all.

The demon Samatos was done feasting off her blood. There was only one thing to do as she lay motionless on the chair. The thing had ordered him to take! Break the deal as she lay unconscious. Take her soul! Rip her flesh from her bones! *Do it now!* The voice said. *Do not come back down here until you do!* Samatos looked around and it was still and quiet and he knew this was the time, now or never! As he ripped piece of her skin off and started to feast on it. He heard a voice saying, *heal her or die!* Samatos ran under the table covered in her blood dripping from his mouth. The voice said louder, *we said, heal her or die!*

Samatos defiant, ordered the voice to go away. "This is not your concern you treacherous vermin! Leave us! She has made her choice."

The voice got angry. *Honour the deal or die!* Samatos knew what it meant. He came from under the table slithering and put the piece of skin back onto her neck where he had ripped it. He placed his hands and healed her.

Just as he did that the devil came appeared before him asking him, "what have you done?"

"He said, they said heal her or die......and I healed her." Samatos was trembling as he said the words.

"At whose authority did you heal her for surely it is not at mine!" The devil was playing games, he knew who and what commanded Samatos, and he was not happy.

Samatos oblivious to the games of his master carried on talking. "They the ones we shall not name who do not exists in this world." The devil stamped his feet 3 times 1......2......3 and on the 3rd stamp hell opened up and demons started to climb from the pits of hell onto the earth right through Karen's living room floor. They came up one by one each bowing to the devil and in turn he nodded to them with his hooves stretched out in front of him. Daharios the strongest and boldest of the demon clan went to Samatos and kicked him down the huge hole into the pits of hell.

Karen who had been unconscious started to wake up, unknowing of the horrors that awaited her. She looked all around her in utter despair and terror that could fill up the ocean. With one big scream she shouted out, "God save me!" But it was too late the demon had decided her fate. The devil had made his choice to break their deal. The deal! The deal that had her calling out for the very being she said did not exist. But did he exist? Did the heavens exists as the hell exists? She wasn't sure anymore but her call was in vain. The demons kept on coming. They kept on coming. Each one worse than the one before it or him.

Suddenly all she heard was a loud scream. A scream so loud that she thought her skin was going to jump out from her body. The scream was so loud that she could no longer hear the scream for she felt that her eardrum had been ripped from her ear and lay on the floor. She don't know what happened next. All she remembers is waking up to an apartment that was back to normal with no demons whatsoever. Was she dreaming? She knows better than to belicve that. She had seen too much already to believe that whole fiasco was a dream. Round 102 goes to the thing; the beast, again! When is she going to win one fight she wonders, and relieve herself from this evil.

"1......2......3, I am not interested in anything but your soul!" That is what kept on playing in her head over and over again. That is what he had said when he first met Karen; the thing.

"1......2......3......what the hell does that mean anyway?" And she found herself asking, "am I really asking the devil for information? All he does is lie! He wouldn't tell me the truth. He has never told me the truth anyway."

"Karen, you called my precious...... Karen you called! You have summoned me for what exactly?"

"I wish to know what one two three means?" Karen was expecting a half-truth.

"It is the number of times I believe it takes for you to render your soul to me." The devil smiled as he said it.

"That is a lie. We had many encounters and you have not had my soul," Karen answered as quickly as his answer to the question she had asked.

"Karen, look around you. I have all souls, and it always takes 1......2......3 appearances for them, the filth we call them in hell. It takes 3 temptations in order for them to surrender everything." The devil was happy to say, starting to enjoy the conversation, the attention it brought him.

"What are the temptations?" Karen was curious now.

"Karen, you know the temptations. You give them a chance to better their life. The first time by offering them an opportunity to screw someone they hate over and show their power. They usually say yes first time with that one. If not, you give them riches to show-off to someone they hate, they usually succumb to that, not realising it is the same thing. For if you seek to get revenge in whatever form, it is revenge. Then you offer them an opportunity to make money by allowing others to suffer."

"How?" Karen said, drawn into the conversation. Like a dance, as the music starts to play and you just cannot stop yourself moving to the beat. She was moving to the beat of the conversation. Taking in its rhythm just waiting for the next song to start so the dance could carry on and wouldn't end.

"By getting them to just focus on the money and ignoring the finer details. No one ever thinks about the finer details Karen, all they hear is, how much can I make?"

"Why is it all about money?" Karen asked.

"Because humans are all about the money." The devil was starting to believe she was stupid at this point. "*What a stupid question*," he thought.

"I am different!" Karen was sure she was not like everybody else.

"Karen honey, you are not different. It just happens you loved something more than the money. And whatever your filth loves the thing knows and changes the scenario to suit."

"You are evil! So, you trick people based on what they really want or love." Karen was angry in herself for falling for the devil's tricks herself.

"I do not make the rules I just execute them. Plus you filth get to choose, remember free will. I am not so bad, you all are the real evil. Killing and maiming each other. You make me look like a saint." He morphed into a saint as he said it to show-off his power.

Karen got really angry with it as she always did in the past. "How dare you call us humans evil! You are the devil for God's sake what is eviller than that you fucking lunatic. Fuck off! Leave me alone already," Karen stormed off into her bedroom leaving the huge snake to slither round the room. The devil opened the pot hole to hell with demons looking up praising his return back to his throne. He knew then, that this world was finally his to do as he please when he please and there is no God to stop him. Finally, the devil had all control to this earth. "*Now how did he get so lucky*," he wondered. As he contemplated the events of the last ten years. He knew he had to go back to the beginning. He opened the big book to look at the world. He flicked through each page and saw the horrors and the wars and the killings and the chaos and general cruelty. He looked and it was good and he found himself starting to be aroused by the chaos and mayhem of his children. Look what he had created, look what his creation had done.

The world was finally his to do with as he pleased. He looked up to the heavens from his pit and his throne and summoned for the Archangel Gabriel to come down. Gabriel obliged and with a quiet entrance into hell sat next to the devil or Lucifer as they called him. The two of them sat side by side as he looked and angel Gabriel looked back and the devil said, "you know there is no way of coming back for him. He no longer exists. This world is mine. Tell him he knows the rules, he must return them to dust in order to lead anything they command."

Gabriel looked at him and said, "our father, never negotiates his creation. Do what you will with this world as they have chosen you to command them but there still remains one, Karen. Karen have not fully chosen, she lies with hope for a win, for something different."

The devil laughed thinking *"this being is delusional."* "Karen has surrendered the world to me on a platter. It was because of Karen you no longer exist in this reality." The devil thought Gabriel had lost his mind with this shit. "Okay tell me the might see it all angel, the one in charge of revelations. What happens next with your so-called Karen? Will she give up her soul just like the rest or not?"

"Karen will be the saviour of this world; Karen will have you crawling back to your pit chained like the beast that you are!" Just as Gabriel finished the words the devil started to strangle him, wrapping his claws around his neck. Archangel Michael knowing how to make a big entrance swooped in and put a sword to the devil's neck warning him that his head would be ripped from his body. The devil apologised, sarcastically, and Michael eased the pressure off the blade.

"Wow, you Archangels cannot take jokes anymore. I was only joking," the devil said, laughing out loud. "Go get out of here you misfits." As Michael led Gabriel away back to heaven. The devil continued to laugh out loud. He took a deep breath and called Samatos and all the other demons in charge of torture and pain. They came in their thousands and they stood before him. The devil said, "they are weak! It is time!" The demon Samatos knew exactly what that meant. It was time to break the rules. Time to challenge their strength, how weak they had become?

CHAPTER 2

Samatos took a step forward and beckoned the demons Solatos and Casilaus to take charge of the clan. One by one they followed marching to their own beat. The ground opened up all over the world. In every city, state and country they continued to march up. It was as if the ground had folded on itself. Samatos was the first one through the gaping hole and he didn't waste time starting to feast on souls. Their skin, muscle and skeletal frame were ripped from their bodies as demons feasted on the spirit; the soul; their essence. As the life drained from them no one knew how or what to say to defend themselves. They were helpless to the devil's power and powerful demons which only purpose was to feed for energy. Some ran into their houses, some hid in cars and on top roofs. Some even climbed trees but there was no hope for any who were alive. For this day would be remembered in history, the day the devil took over the earth and consumed human beings as soup.

Karen looked out of her window and couldn't believe what she was seeing. It had begun. Her deal with the devil had finally come about. The pain she felt could overpower an elephant, the guilt, the shame was too much for her to stay living. She began to cut her wrist with the butter knife that was in her hand. Blood started to run down her wrist dripping into her palm. It was just a flesh wound, but her being overdramatic, she passed out.

"Karen, wake up, beautiful!" She heard a voice calling out to her, "wake up Karen!" She opened her eyes slightly, her head sore from the fall. All she saw for a split second was her dead mother leaning over her. "Karen wake up! The world needs you more than ever!" Karen instantly got up remembering the pact she had made with the devil. She needed to get to the Care home straight away.

She arrived at the Care home about 12:03pm and everyone seemed oblivious to the chaos outside and she couldn't understand why. As she walked into the home further she could see Marla staring outside through the curtains. "They are coming to get us aren't they? They will rip our souls from our body."

Karen hugged her. "No they cannot. I made a deal I sorted it all out for us!"

Marla looked at her and smiled, "you cannot sort this out dear. They did this. We have given the world to hell." Marla turned from Karen and continued to look at the mayhem of souls screaming for their lives.

Karen started to call to God, the one that does not exist, still not believing she would get any response at all. "I don't know where you are but you cannot let this happen. This world may not be brilliant. I know we have done a lot of bad things but give us another chance. It is too much. Do you not see what he is doing, stop him!" A thought appeared in Karen's head, *"no you stop it. Karen your deal is the key, or everyone and everything will perish right before your eyes, even God himself."* Karen not realising her call to God had been answered; as a thought. Felt God really no longer existed and she was now reasoning with herself through her own understanding of the last 6 years. Karen started to cry. "I cannot break the deal! The deal is sealed in my blood. What if I break the deal and I die and they all die. I need to protect the residents they are all I have left."

Karen had been working in the Care home as a nurse for 7 years. All she remembers is the residents bringing joy to her heart and soul. She loved them. They were her family. Karen heard 'the thing' coming; her word for the demon that visited her and the devil. She said to Marla, "no matter what, do not let it know you can see it, please I beg you!"

Marla looked at her and said, "honey he is the devil he knows everything." Karen couldn't help but smile at the wise resident who seem to know all and see all. 'The thing' approached surrounded by the clan of demons. They headed to the front door of the Care home, like a clan they formed a circle and waited for Karen. They had no choice but to honour the deal. The residents of Oakin Grove to carry on living their comfortable life. Karen never asked for her soul to be saved she only asked for the residents of her beloved Care home. Marla who Karen was pretty fond of and the rest of the residents who in Karen's opinion had lived their life, dedicated their life to this country and she would not have them die such a brutal death.

She was told by the thing *"in order to save your beloved residents you must bleed when I say you bleed, you must allow them to feed on your flesh until it is time."* What she didn't realise is there cannot be salvation without sacrifice, and as she bled each time, she created a countdown to the destruction of the world. At any time, she could have stopped this madness; not adhered to the thing's request but she thought she was doing what was right for herself and the residents. The countdown was over, the world was darkness's world and Karen had helped it be this way.

What remained was the deal, could the deal stick, could the world carry on in some way with the residents of Oakin, and how? How could Karen stop this madness and could it be stopped. The clan stood there staring at her and Marla. One demon laughed and said, "we see you brought back-up."

Marla laughed back sarcastically, "I used to be a black belt in my young days watch out how you speak to me."

Samatos the demon snapped back at her, "but now you are in a wheelchair you old fool!"

The devil raised his hands to shut Samatos up. "Enough talking!" He said angrily. "I have come to honour our deal with some conditions." He pulled out the scroll that Karen had signed and pointed to section 5:23. He repeated; "section 5:23 states in order for the deal to be maintained you must sacrifice one resident." Karen laughed, thinking this was a joke. The document she signed never said that.

"You are a liar! It never said that, you added that in." The devil pulled Karen close to him morphing back into his true form, going from a 4-legged beast, thangs out over his teeth with his mouth elongated. Now he was towering over her on two legs chest puffed out with a crown appearing instantly on his head.

"I am the king of this deal and I say one sacrifice has to be given to keep the deal." The devil clearly knew he had the upper hand.

Karen refused, "over my dead body! Honour the deal now or I take it back."

"Karen you cannot take the deal back it is set. Read here it says one soul must be willingly sacrificed in order that the rest can be saved." Karen saw at the bottom in very tiny, tiny writing it did say that, but how could anyone notice that as part of the contract. She felt she had been fooled all this time; they were all going to die. It's one soul today but what about tomorrow and the next day, it will never end. The thing stood there staring at Karen, "what will it be? Who have you chosen?"

"I cannot choose they have to choose for themselves. I thought everyone had free will." Karen was trying to reason with the devil, now she knew she was desperate.

"Oh, dear sweet Karen they have already chosen. You are just here to offer the sacrifice in your name are you not. You are the queen of this deal after all, so which will it be? The old one next to you or will you pick one you are less fond of; it is your decision. I am just here to make it all happen."

"I will not choose, I tell you! Do what you want to do but it will not be by my hand. This Care home is supposed to be free from this nightmare, this chaos, you promised!"

"I promised no such thing. I promised that your residents will not be harmed and they will not. If you give one to save the rest."

"It is a waste of my time and energy talking to you. I am going back into that Care home and you will not enter here because you cannot because that was the deal. You are not allowed to come in here, we are on sacred ground."

"There is no such thing as sacred ground. Look around you Karen, you are in hell. This is hell on earth. Humans' worst nightmare, yes." The beast knew Karen was right the deal meant he could not enter the Care home but he was not going to give her any confidence at this point. The mission was to break her spirits and watch her surrender her soul to him willingly.

He was starting to scare her and Karen just wanted to make sure all her residents were safe in the Care home. "*This beast always has something up his sleeves*," she thought. She ran back into the home, frantically checking on each resident making sure they were all in their rooms or somewhere on the grounds away from the devil. All residents apart from one were accounted for. Simon was missing. Simon was the storyteller of the Care home always willing to sit down and read a story to his fellow residents. Karen started to freak-out checking everywhere, knocking on all toilet doors and bathroom doors but to no avail. Simon was not in the home.

She decided to look outside through Marla's bedroom window which was facing the street and the front door. Karen saw Simon. He was heading towards the home oblivious to the horrors around him. Why could Simon not see the demons and the chaos surrounding every step? Because Karen made a deal with the devil. "*When the time comes for you to take over the world, please spare the residents of the Care home they cannot see or hear any of this. They are frail and may die just from the shock of it all.*" But Marla could see the horrors and Karen did not know why.

As Simon walked up the road towards the home Karen knew she had to get to the front door before he did. She ran down the stairs as if her life depended on it. Once she got to the front entrance Simon was not there and neither was the devil or his demons. She knew straight away that the beast had gotten his sacrifice. She knelt down in front of the Care home and started to pray. Something she had not done in a long time. "I apologise if I have not believed in you, and apologise if I have forgotten about you but I need you now. I cannot do this on my own, I am lost sorry." As Karen finished the words Archangel Gabriel appeared before her with the whitest wings she had ever seen and a gold halo and eyes white as snow with gold pupils and a Gold and white cloak with gold sandals. Gabriel spoke with an echo, "Karen you are not alone!"

Karen could not believe her eyes or ears for this could not be real, "I called and you came; that simple. Are you kidding me! Where the hell have you all been all this time?" Karen, attacked the Archangel and started to punch at the being before her. As she hit all she was hitting was stone and she realised Gabriel no longer stood before her but it was Archangel Michael.

"Are you going to stop or must we make you stop." Michael was taking charge of her hysterics before it got out of control. Karen stopped instantly, tired from the exertion, looking at her knuckles, to realise there was no bruise or pain or redness.

She asked Michael, "did he heal me?"

"Who are you talking about?" Michael wanted to have fun to lighten the situation.

Karen was only frustrated by his attempt; "oh my gosh! are you slow or something! God! I mean did God heal me?"

Michael laughed, "there is no God remember!" Karen was annoyed now. She had just lost a resident and here was this being mocking her at such a crucial time, now, at the end of the world.

"Well anyway why are you here, then?" Karen didn't see the point now of this great being now here and not living up to its name.

"You called Karen." Gabriel answered, realising Karen had gotten bored with Michael's attempts at changing her energy, trying to get her to put things into perspective without the crazy talk in her head of ego.

"I called to God not you and therefore if he does exist, why did you come?" Karen wanted justification from this so-called God.

"Exactly, said Archangel Michael. So there lies the answer to your question."

"Oh my gosh! Are angels always so philosophical. Is God here or not? Did he send you? and if he did what do you plan on doing about this chaos? People are dead! You better go do something, now!" Karen was now ordering the Archangels, well someone had to take control of the situation and she thought she was doing that.

"There is nothing to do Karen you all have decided your fate the world has been given over to the dark. We only come because you called for help." Michael wanted her to finally put things into perspective. This was indeed the end for mankind, well the mankind that existed now, that is. Things could not exist anymore in the world Karen knew and loved and wanted to carry on for the sake of her residents.

"What the fuck are you talking about! You are a fucking Archangel! Go fight, go do something! Did you not order Lucifer from heaven or something, aren't you the badass of all God's angels. Go save the world." Karen was scared and the fear was manifesting itself as; anger in the angels.

"No one have asked." Michael kept his cool, for now!

"Fuck it! I am asking! Go take it back now!" Karen knew she was pushing it. Her tone was unbearable, but if that is what it took for them to get off their ass after so long of doing nothing, she was going to take it as far as they allowed her to. She was not stupid, just scared shitless.

"Karen, calm down. Your disrespect is wearing thin and my father grows angry." Gabriel tried to reason with her.

"Let him grow angry. Maybe he needs to get angry to get off his ass and do something," Karen screamed at the sky, "Do Something! Do you hear me! Do something!"

Now with a hoarse voice Karen knelt down defeated from the extra use of energy. As she looked up Archangel Michael and Archangel Gabriel no longer stood before her. What stood before her was a grand oak tree. The biggest and tallest oak tree she had ever seen. This tree was no ordinary tree. This tree spoke and the words Karen could barely hear but she heard it just enough to comply with its wishes. The tree said softly, "*climb me.*" Karen instinctively started to climb. She didn't pause or think about it, she just started to climb. The more she climbed the more energy she got to keep climbing. Once she had got a quarter way the tree said, "*now fall.*" Karen took a moment. Did she really hear that. She listened more closely and indeed the words were, "*now fall. You wish to see me then fall.*"

Karen knew who it was. She fell! As she fell she had accepted death would come and indeed death did come. She fell and broke every bone in her body and was taken up to heaven and was seated at the head of the table in a white place. It couldn't be classed as a room. It was a white open space. The table was white and didn't appear to be there but once you rest your hands it appeared. On the right side of the room close to the disappearing table was a four-legged beast with 7 eyes, yellow eyes with black pupils. On the left side there was a half-eaten fish floating in the air with a gold crown and beams of light all around it. It floated towards her and she moved back scared. The fish said, "why are you scared Karen? This is home." Karen didn't understand. Was she dead and would not be returning to earth, is that it.

A voice came from the end of the table but she could not see anything. The light was too bright that she could not look at it. The voice said, "Karen you asked for me now here I am." The bright light suddenly disappeared and what stood before her was a man. A bone and flesh man.

She couldn't understand, God was a man. This made no sense to her. She asked, "who are you?"

"I go by many names Karen, the alpha, the omega. I am who and what you seek. I am here as you asked."

"You are telling me you are God. The God that made the earth. You are a man, a white man, that makes it worse!" Karen was disappointed. She was convinced she should have not bothered climbing the oak tree.

"Karen dear, I am whatever you need me to be." God was being polite.

"I need you to be you. Come in your true form." Karen wasn't prepared to talk to a white man about this. It didn't seem like she was really in heaven otherwise.

"What form is that Karen?" God was interested in her answer; whatever it was.

"I don't know. Like a great big animal or I don't know; something big." Karen was expecting something grander.

"I did come as something big; the oak tree." God said.

"So, you take many forms?" Karen asked, feeling a bit better now about climbing that tree.

"I am everything Karen." God was expecting the questions she asked.

"Am I dead?" Karen had to ask.

"If you want to be then you are. You have a choice. You can stay here with us or go back to fix earth." Could any of it be fixed? that was the question. "Make another choice, Karen. Choose light over dark, and you will be instructed what to do to save earth and stop this massacre of you all."

"Okay so what do I do?" Karen asked.

"First thing, you have to go back." Karen was forced from heaven with one push from God. She found herself in her body once more but not on a pavement, instead in her bedroom lying in bed. As she lay in bed she felt like a different person. Like she wasn't herself. She decided to get up, and started to draw what she had seen as not to forget anything. As she drew, all the pages started to come alive. The beings came out from the page and stood before her. As they stood, she wondered what she had done to this world. If that is all it took to summon light, how did she end up summoning the devil instead. But there was no time to contemplate the past. She asked the beings that stood before her why they were there.

"You asked for help Karen and we're here to help." They all answered together.

"There are only 4 of you. There are thousands of demons roaming the streets all around the world, how are you going to stop them all?" The half-eaten fish; meaning the being with just a fish head, fish bones in the middle and a fish tail spoke first and said, "Karen fear not with us comes 10,000 men. For one Archangel comes with the strength of 10,000 and we come with an Archangel protecting each of us and leading us. Karen didn't feel safer sorry. She analysed the beings before her and they didn't look powerful enough, sorry. The second being she had drawn was a spider with red legs but a human face; a white as snow female face, beautiful in the face but creepy when it crawled. It confused her, were these beings from God or the devil they looked really weird. The third being was half horse and half man and she wondered, what is this obsession with human and animal. The only being who seems whole to her and not confused was the 4-legged beast with seven eyes. He seemed like he could defend himself.

She opened her curtains and showed them the horrors that were happening despite their so-called power. God no longer was in control of this world humans had handed it over on a plate to the devil and it was never going to be the same again. The half-eaten fish with light beaming from it flew down and flung its tail at one of the demons who was feasting on a woman's flesh with her baby crying in the pram next to her. The demon as if it had been hit indeed by 10,000 men and an Archangel flew into the sky for what seemed to be an eternity before crashing down to the ground creating a big pot hole into hell. At that point the other Godly creatures joined the being with the fish head and half eaten fish body and started to pound on the other demons kicking them into the pit. For what seemed to be hours. Karen was staring from her window behind the curtains cheering them on.

"Karen, the deal, Karen." A voice came from the sofa behind her. It was the devil himself, in human form, sitting on the sofa eating an apple with a knife in his left hand. "Karen the deal, you signed in section 33:66. It specifically said, no Godly interference at all. You made the deal Karen."

"I didn't state I would never contact Godly creatures I stated they did not exist. They exist and therefore this changes the notion of the contract," Karen was beginning to get smart. Indeed, the devil looked at what was said and with a huff and a puff and his belly swelling up 'the thing' spanned around and vanished right before her eyes. Karen thought to herself that will teach him. She may just be able to be free from this deal after all. Something told her that, that was not going to be as easy as she thought though.

The Godly beings returned looking like they hadn't broke a sweat and Karen wanted to know what was going to happen now. How was God going to fix this mess, this horror on earth. Stop this killing of humans. Karen was sure they had a plan. "Sorry there is no plan Karen. You handed the world to Lucifer and that means demons can now populate this physical plane when they couldn't before. You have given them the authority to make earth hell. A new order is being created where the devil owns earth instead of God," the half-eaten fish said.

"Are you crazy! That is not possible. God created everything the stars and the moon and the sun he owns everything." Karen found it hard to take in what they were saying.

"Well Karen a few moments ago you didn't believe God even exist. Now imagine how it has been the last 10 years humans not believing God exist all over the world. Some countries are better than others but the consensus is the same; you believe the devil's power is stronger than God. You have accepted that in your heart and your soul which means you have made it so. The devil just chose you to sign on the dotted line so this process would happen quicker, but this was inevitable." The half horse half man explained.

"How did I make it happen quicker?" Karen asked.

"Because you promised him, he could have this world if he spared the residents of the Care home you worked in," fish-head said.

"I thought it meant everything I owned. I said everything I own, not the world. Then it became not enough and I just blurted it out. I never meant to say the world. He just always came for more and more; he was never satisfied. What do I do now can I not take it back." Karen was filled with guilt.

"Karen what has been done cannot be undone. What we can do is work with what we have. The Care home is safe and therefore our safe haven. But understand we are limited because of your deal. We can only challenge demons when you give us direct permission to, in order to do that you must be with us and think us or speak us to help you and others," the fish-head made it clearer to her.

"Just great, so how long is that going to take? This shit is happening all around the world as we speak. We cannot bc all around the world." Karen was making sense.

"Let us start with just England Karen, that's where we are now after all," fish-head was making even more sense.

Karen was fuming she was thinking what kind of angels or Godly creatures are these why can't they just wipe out the demons. She needed to get back to the Care home she hated this shit, nothing is going to be done but at least the residents were safe that's the main thing. As Karen said that she felt this overwhelming feeling to jump out of the window. She didn't know where and when this feeling came but the urge was great, so great that she found herself holding on to the refrigerator next to her. The beings standing there knew what it was. She was changing and she didn't even know that she was, but changing into what exactly what was she changing to, that was the question. The thing is Karen did not understand her gift, the gift that she had; the ability to walk between worlds. The ability to be on this physical plane on earth but also her spirit was able to leave her body and travel to the underworld and also heaven.

Karen didn't understand her deal meant she gave up her Soul to the devil and had to go through a series of tests and growth in order to get it back. The series of tests would leave her not as Karen but as someone and something more. Karen was not interested in hearing any more today she was more interested in resting and didn't want to tell the other beings how she felt not knowing that they already knew what was going on. She didn't have to say anything to them they knew everything. They were from God after all, because they were from God, they saw what he saw and heard what he heard because he allowed them to. They didn't say anything to Karen because she had to ask for more information and she didn't ask and as she didn't ask there wasn't much, they could do. They knew to receive she had to ask, to ask it was to receive, and as they knew all that, they waited for her to ask for all the information in order for them to tell.

CHAPTER 3

Karen had not known the way things worked because she was so consumed with everything she had once knew about this world that she didn't know any different than what she had been told. All she was told is what the devil wanted her to know in order to get her to do what he wanted her to do. Karen had always been a bit gullible even as a child. Now at the age of 35 she found herself believing more than believing less. She gave people the benefit of the doubt despite them not giving her any reason to give them the benefit of the doubt; she did. When the devil first approached Karen all she could do was stand there, she didn't know what to say or what to do. After all who knows what to say to the devil. Who is prepared for something like that. Who says the day I meet the devil I will be telling him this and that, who knows how to react in these situations. Karen was disappointed in herself for believing anything she was told. Now she was going to ask questions, now she was going to tell everyone what she thought including God as well. Fuck being this weak bitch! She was going to stand up to all these fuckers. She was going to speak up now and say what she really feels about everything. She was going to rescue the world with her voice, with her words. Tell everyone how fucked up this world is with the devil controlling everything. She was going to speak up now so people can save their lives from this bullshit.

As Karen made this decision to speak out, she wondered if the devil would decide to pay her a visit trying to show her who is really in charge of this world and who would carry on running things here now that he was in charge and God was no more. Karen didn't wish to acknowledge the devil and certainly didn't want to accept that things had gotten this bad and she was the cause of it. "Fuck off! This isn't my fault they all chose this with their hatred for each other." She went to her secret drawer and pulled out all horrible news stories written in the last year of crimes by the public as well as government fraud claims. She was not going to accept that she could choose for everyone. What ever happened to fucking accountability. Why was she the monster here. She just wanted to be left alone at this point. She was not willing to be the scapegoat, everyone did and had to play their part. As far as she was concerned this was not all down to her at all. Karen was just fed up of all of it she just wanted to get away from it all like it never happened.

Karen knew she was making a bad situation worse with the blaming game. At the end of the day everyone has their part to play including her and focusing on others was wasting time. She knew she had to put a plan into working out how she was going to fix this mess everyone created. One thing she learned from the devil is humans always blame other people for the choices they make. It is always someone else's fault. She didn't want to be that person. She had to accept her part and be kind to herself that she didn't really understand what she was choosing, she got played from her fears. The devil manipulated her and now she had God here and they were going to fix things. "*I mean if God cannot help then who can right.*" As, she said that in her head she thought of her friend Gordon and knew he could help. She hadn't spoken to him for years but she knew he knew a lot about God and hell and he was always talking about things she never understood in the past. But some of it was starting to make sense based on what the devil was and had said. She decided she was going to pay Gordon a visit and the Godly creatures were going to come with her. Now telling them may be a problem but she would see. She called to Archangel Gabriel to come down.

"Okay guys. I know a lot is going on and I have been a little bit of an ass. But I have a plan. You asked me to fix this right.... so, I have this friend and he knows a lot about this stuff. He may understand more of what you all are saying than I do. Can you come when I pay him a visit?" Gabriel answered yes, knowing who Karen was referring to.

The drive took Karen a while but when she finally got there, she could see this was the worse idea she had in a long time. Gordon was sitting on his porch drinking a beer with his legs stretched out as if he had no care in the world. She wondered whether he was oblivious to the chaos around him or what; "*what the hell is this shit, get off your ass and do something. What the fuck was he doing.*" Karen was tempted to say all this out loud. She really was pissed now, before even uttering a word she was angry with him already. "Hi Gordon."

"Wow, Karen long time no see! You must have been what 23 the last time I saw you, how are things?" He was seeming less of an arsehole he did welcome her after all.

"Well Gordon, I made a pact with the devil and now demons are roaming the street and ripping people's face apart sucking their souls from their body and I lost a resident and the Care home is supposed to be safe now but it is not. I summoned God but then God said I needed to fix it so here I am needing your help please, tell me you can help me!"

Gordon looked at her, and said, "Karen I cannot help you. Look around you. This place is peaceful. Do you see a demon in sight. I have everything I need right here. Karen I made a deal. I am so pleased I did. Sorry if your deal didn't work out but that is too bad for you. I got everything I wanted honey. But if you are willing to show me a good time then I am willing to share my expertise with you. I have had many conversations with him the big guy and I can tell you what you need to do to save yourself and your pre-cious Care home."

"What you have had conversations with God?" She looked at him up and down and thought no way he was telling the truth about speaking to God, he reeked of alcohol for one. The place was a tip; not even a homeless person would feel comfortable in this filth. He called this a home; "*yuck!*" she thought. She would catch something just by standing in his sitting room. She wanted to ask him what deal he made but she was too scared to. She wanted to call on to God as they agreed to be there with her, to change his mind, but she could tell he was consumed by the dark and couldn't be reasoned with. So that was it for her she had no one on earth to help her she had to do this shit by herself. Fuck Gordon and his filthy house she was going to deal with this herself it was her mess and she was going to deal with it one way or another. So there she was finally getting it that no one on earth could help but God himself.

She turned over to Gordon and said, "you piece of shit all this time I blamed myself for what is happening and it is vermin like you that caused this."

"Don't get all righteous with me lady. What bout you and your deal. I mean who is the fuckup? you or me! You made a deal and asked nothing for yourself. Look at me I am living in luxury." He, went to his bedroom, as Karen wanted to see what he was talking about she followed him. As he opened the door she couldn't believe her eyes his bedroom was filled with gold bars. Karen looked at the sight of it and couldn't contain herself; she leaped at him digging her nails into his eyes.

"You piece of shit! Where the fuck are you spending this shit if everyone is gone! Who the fuck are you buying from! Do you not see the shit going on out there! She couldn't stop hitting him, punching him in the face. He grabbed her by her neck, threw her on to the floor and started to squeeze her throat.

"*I am going to kill this bitch*," that's all he could think about as he squeezed the life out of her.

She couldn't die like this, she called, "Gabriel, Michael…… anyone help!" Michael stood over them both and stretched out his hand and the grip on her neck loosened as if it was not there. Michael had healed Gordon's face and Karen's abrasions on her neck. "There is enough fighting you two must stop it now, this is not going to help the situation." Karen remained laying down still feeling the effects of being choked. Gordon just knelt there in shock at what he was seeing. Seeing the devil in its true form is one thing but seeing this was utterly amazing. But then the fear hit him, if this was God then he was in trouble because he had sold his soul to the devil. He started to panic and he put his own thought to the devil, calling to the demon Samatos to destroy them, to get rid of what stood in his house.

Samatos obliged and came up, ordering Michael to leave. Michael reminded him of the rules and laws. If a being calls even by just a thought; God stays as long as he is needed. Samatos equally reminded Michael that the same rule applies to darkness. Michael bowed low to the demon that stood before him and said, "make us leave! You spawn of Lucifer!"

At, that point the devil appeared before Michael, and said, "no you make me leave!" A fight broke out in Gordon's corridor. With both beings showing their strength and might. All that was missing Karen thought was for God to join the party. She was loving how Michael was getting the upper hand over the devil, this was cool.

All she heard next was a voice saying, "*Michael stop it this is beneath you*!" Michael stopped instantly. Karen was disappointed, it was getting good. Gordon's living room was even more of a tip and she was loving it. There were big holes in the ceiling and the floor from the fire balls that came down from heaven, as Michael aimed at the devil's head with his laser sword. This shit was fucking exciting. The heavens and hell had unleased onto the earth and she knew that light was going to win over the dark.

"*God was a badass,*" she thought. But as that thought came it vanished God ordered Michael to return to the skies. She thought, "*what the fuck is this*!" As Michael leaped into the air. The devil too slithered down to his pit. Leaving Karen with this piece of shit Gordon and the demon Samatos bleeding in the corner. One of the fireballs summoned by Michael had ripped him into half. As Karen watched him die on Gordon's living room floor she realised why God had summoned the Archangel home. She remembered what the devil had told her, "*your God is predictable. He will not take his creation as sacrifice. He loves humans too much to destroy them at will. He will always hold on to the notion you all will eventually choose each other; at the pain and suffering of each other.*" Samatos lifeless body lay there as a casualty of war and she realised that could have been a human being and God was not willing to have them as sacrifices. Unwilling sacrifices through thoughts and feelings they were not fully aware they had but were just leading each blindly to death. As Samatos lay there with the devil not claiming him as his own for disappointing him. Karen reached down to pick up the demon's bodies, each piece hollow and empty. She decided she would bury the bodies in the garden. Gordon wasn't having none of it. "I am not having that thing buried here! Are you kidding me! What if it rose back up aren't these things magical or something. It may wake up from the dead or something."

"So you will spend time with the devil and make a deal and take his money but you will not spend time with a body that is harmless now as it is dead. Are you fucking blind! Can you not see it is dead!" Karen was having none of his bullshit.

"The question is why the fuck do you want to bury it?" Gordon was ready to rip her head from her body, he was that angry. "Haven't you picked your side or are you confused or something!" Gordon was confused by her so-called good deed focused at helping darkness find closure. Who the fuck chooses to bury a demon, she was crazy.

"I am not confused Gordon, but in this world of fucking hatred. We need some love, positivity, isn't that how this spreads. You keep bringing negativity and it is like a ripple effect it goes around. You spread positivity and everyone feeds off that."

"Okay, and how did that work out so far. Look at the world we are living in, it is a shithole. Fucking negative! No one gives a fuck about anyone and anything. At the end of the day humans are fucked up. Fuck everyone up I say before they fuck you up." Gordon was not giving up; it was his house.

"You know that's how we got here in the first place with the fucking devil owning the world because everyone chose to not give a fuck about anyone and anything other than getting paid." Karen felt this had to be done to raise the energy of the world.

"Well, that is life who doesn't want to get paid." He opened the door to his bedroom once more as he said it. Karen had heard enough all she wanted to do was get the fuck out of that house. That is exactly what she did dragging the demon outside with her. As she dragged it, she could swear it was getting heavier and heavier. So heavy that she had to stop to take a breath. As she started up again; the demon would not move. It was as if someone glued it to the ground. She kept on pulling but nothing happened, no movement at all.

A voice came from the heavens that said, "let it be Karen. Lucifer is not allowing this to happen, save your energy for the real fight."

Karen thought, "*well what the fuck is the real fight! This was the fight*." She didn't get what was the real fight. She didn't get it at all. But she stopped pulling. As she stopped the ground opened up below the demon and sucked him into it and quickly shut back up. Karen thought to herself, "*fucking bastard. He will not let one good deed happen*." She realised how dumb she was and dumb everyone else was to allow this to happen, to allow the devil to have this world. There was not one kind bone in his body and she understood why the world was this bad, why no one was kind anymore and why they were all so mean to each other and cared less about each other. She realised in that moment humans were the devil himself we were no longer in God's likeness. We were more like demons and the devil. The thought of it all made her sick. She threw up on the grass in Gordon's back garden, and passed out.